LACROSSE
FIRESTORM

THE #1
SPORTS SERIES
FOR KIDS

LACROSSE
FIRESTORM

Text by Stephanie Peters

LITTLE, BROWN AND COMPANY
NEW YORK BOSTON

Copyright © 2008 by Matt Christopher Royalties, Inc.

Little, Brown and Company

Hachette Book Group
1290 Avenue of the Americas, New York, NY 10104
Visit our website at www.lb-kids.com

www.mattchristopher.com

Little, Brown and Company is a division of Hachette Book Group, Inc.
The Little, Brown name and logo are trademarks of Hachette Book Group, Inc.

The publisher is not responsible for websites (or their content)
that are not owned by the publisher.

First Edition: April 2008

Matt Christopher® is a registered trademark of Matt Christopher Royalties, Inc.

ISBN-13: 978-0-316-01631-5

Text written by Stephanie True Peters

LACROSSE
FIRESTORM

1

What's *with* you, Wallis? Haven't you ever held a lacrosse stick before?"

Garry Wallis shot an angry look at Michael Donofrio. He knew he should be used to his teammate's big mouth; after all, Michael was always ridiculing someone on the Rockets.

Usually, however, that someone was Garry's brother, Todd. Todd had never played lacrosse until last spring. Then, he only joined the Rockets to get some exercise and lose weight. At first, he was terrible, but thanks to some help from the coach's son, Jeff Hasbrouck, he began to improve.

1

But that didn't stop Michael from bullying him. He thought Todd was dragging the team down — "dead weight," Michael called him, a jab at Todd's size as well as his lack of skill — and he all but ordered Garry to force his brother to quit. When Garry refused, Michael took matters into his own hands and slashed the webbing of Todd's stick before a game!

That's when Garry decided it was time to put Michael in his place. He knew Michael had set his sights on winning the league's top scorer award; he wanted to make sure Michael didn't get it. Since plenty of other Rockets were sick of Michael's attitude too, they helped Garry with his "don't pass to Michael" plan.

Michael was furious when he realized that no one was feeding him the ball. His anger grew when, at the season's end, he wasn't the league's top scorer.

"I know you're behind it," he had snarled at Garry after the last game. "And I'll make you pay!"

After that, Garry had avoided Michael as best he could. Unfortunately, for the next week, he and Michael would be together day and night.

The Rockets were taking part in a lacrosse tournament held at an overnight camp. And it was clear that Michael planned to take every opportunity to make Garry's life miserable.

Like now.

The Rockets were playing the Cougars in the first round of the two-game elimination tournament. It was the middle of the third quarter and the Cougars led, 9–7. The Rockets needed to pull ahead; if they lost this game, and then one more, they would be watching the rest of the tourney from the sidelines.

Garry was usually one of the Rockets' better players. But right now, he was very tired — and not just from the exertion of the game. He hadn't slept well the night before.

Garry was sharing a four-bunk cabin with Todd, Jeff, and another boy named Conor. Conor was a fun kid and a decent player, but he had one annoying trait: he snored all night long!

Todd and Jeff weren't bothered by the noise because their bunk beds were on the other side of the cabin. Garry, however, was right above Conor and for the past two nights he'd heard every last snort, nose whistle, wheeze, and rumble.

"It's like someone's turning a chain saw on and off next to my ear," Garry whispered to Todd and Jeff at breakfast that morning. "I can't believe you guys don't hear it!"

"So jam something in your ears at night," Todd suggested.

"Like what, my fingers?"

"No, like earplugs," Todd replied. "I'll bet the health center has some."

Garry nodded thoughtfully. "That's not a bad idea, actually. And if they don't, I'll wad up some toilet paper and stick that in!"

"Just be sure it's nice *new* toilet paper!" Jeff joked.

Garry got the earplugs later that morning. He stuck them in his sweatshirt pocket with a silent prayer that they'd help him sleep better — and hopefully, wake up rested and back to his usual playing form. For right now, Garry was messing up badly and giving Michael all the ammunition he needed to ridicule him on the field.

2

Thanks to Garry's lousy throw, the Cougars had possession of the ball and were running with it down the sidelines. Their left wing attacker was stocky but surprisingly fast. He cradled the ball to one side of his body and held out his arm to block any oncoming attacks.

Carl and Eric, two of the Rockets defensemen, formed just such an offensive. They charged the attacker together, stopping him in his tracks.

The Cougar whirled and looked for someone to pass to. He found his center midfielder in the clear and slashed his stick downward to send the ball his way.

Whap! Jeff, the Rockets center middie, anticipated the throw and slapped the ball down to the ground before the Cougar could reach it. The ball bounced through the grass toward Samuel, another Rockets midfielder. Samuel stuck his stick under it and scooped it up. Now the action was headed toward the Cougars goal!

"Pass it up, already!" Michael screamed.

Samuel did, a line drive bomb that socked right into the pocket of Michael's stick.

Michael cradled it, spun around, and dashed toward the crease.

A Cougars defenseman challenged him but then fell back a step when Michael didn't slow down.

"Can't see!" the Cougars goalkeeper yelled.

That was all the advantage Michael needed. He sidestepped past the defenseman and blasted a vicious shot toward the net. The goalkeeper saw the ball coming and lunged to make the save, but was just a moment too late.

Goal!

The Rockets cheered and whooped. Michael acknowledged the praise with a fist pumped in the air. Then he ambled back to the center X for the face-off. He passed Garry on the way.

"Wallis, since you're not doing diddly out there today," he growled, "just feed me the ball and get out of my way. Got it?"

"I'd rather eat my stick!" Garry snarled back.

"Really? See me after the game and I'll feed it to you myself!"

"Good one, D-man," Evan, the Rockets left midfielder, called. Evan was Michael's sidekick. Lately, he seemed to be trying to curry Michael's favor by giving him different nicknames. It hadn't worked as far as Garry could tell. Michael still treated Evan like a lower life-form.

Jeff ran up behind them. "Knock it off, you guys," he said to Garry and Michael, "and start acting like teammates, will you?"

The two boys exchanged one last angry look. Then Garry moved to the wing area and Michael to the center. The referee put the ball on the X, stepped back, and blew his whistle.

Michael flipped his stick over the ball, twisted the head around, and sent the ball bounding over to Conor on the right.

"Weave!" he cried, the call for a three-man passing play down the field.

Conor snatched the ball from the grass and immediately started running toward the center of the field. As he did, Michael came toward him. Garry, meanwhile, prepared to receive the ball from Conor and then take his place in the center.

But Michael had other ideas. "Garry's covered!" he yelled to Conor. "Pass back!"

Conor didn't bother to look Garry's way to see if Michael was telling the truth. If he had, he would have seen that Garry had dodged past his defender and was, in fact, completely open.

Darn that Michael! Garry thought furiously as he watched Michael get the ball back from Conor. *The weave would have worked if he wasn't so selfish!*

When two defenders stormed Michael from either side and broke up his attack, Garry couldn't help grinning — even though it meant the Rockets had missed out on a chance to score. Luckily, the Cougars bobbled their goal attempt and the Rockets reclaimed possession. Two minutes and some quick passes later, the ball was in the Cougars net!

The third quarter ended with the Rockets within one goal of a win.

Coach Hasbrouck gave them a rousing pep talk during the short break and sent them back onto the field. Every Rocket out there was determined to take the game away from the Cougars.

But as the clock ticked downward, the score remained tied. Ten minutes to go. Five. And still it stood at Cougars 9, Rockets 9.

Then the Rockets got a lucky break. A Cougars defender, thinking Evan had the ball, slammed into the middie from behind.

Tweet! The referee blew a blast on his whistle and pointed a finger at the Cougar. "Illegal body check! One minute penalty!" he shouted.

Coach Hasbrouck clapped madly from the sidelines. "Power play! Now's your chance, Rockets!"

With two minutes left to go, the Cougars were one man down on the field. The Rockets front line went into action. Garry, Michael, and Conor charged to the crease. Jeff sent the ball to Samuel, who carried it past the midfield line and rocketed it to Conor. Conor flashed a quick, sharp shot to Michael. Michael turned on his heel as if to pass to Garry — only to turn back, square up to the goal, and fake a shot. Evan streaked up behind Garry and received Michael's pass. Michael then dashed across the crease in front of Garry, and held up his stick for a return pass.

It was a tricky maneuver, one that called for Evan to make a perfect pass around Garry.

Unfortunately, Evan's pass was far from perfect. Instead of landing in Michael's pocket, the ball flew over his head and right into the webbing of the goalie's oversize stick head.

"Oh, good going, Wallis!" Evan fumed as they hustled back to help out the defense.

"What're you blaming me for?" Garry returned angrily.

"You got in my way so I couldn't see Michael!"

"Then you shouldn't have tried passing to him!" Garry argued.

"Heads up!" Jeff's warning came a second too late.

Blam! The hard rubber lacrosse ball struck Garry right in the helmet! He saw stars as he fell to the ground. Then he saw a stick reach past him and scoop up the ball. He wobbled to his feet just in time to see Michael race down the field, twist past two defenders, and put the ball in the net — moments before the buzzer sounded to end the game!

13

The Rockets had won! They whooped, belly-bumped each other, and slapped jumping high fives. Todd helped his brother to his feet and Garry celebrated along with his teammates — even though his head was ringing.

"Man," he finally asked Jeff and Todd, "who threw that?"

Jeff started to answer but was interrupted.

"Nice assist, Wallis," Michael drawled. "If I'd known you could use your head that way, I would have ricocheted one off your helmet long ago!" Laughing, he sauntered away to receive his teammates' congratulations.

Garry stared from his brother to Jeff and back again. "Michael threw that ball at my head on purpose, didn't he?" he demanded.

"Garry, come on, it must have been an accident," Jeff said.

"Had to have been," Todd put in, "Michael wouldn't —"

"Oh, he would, and you know it!" Garry was so angry he spat the words. "I can't believe you, Todd, of all people, are sticking up for him! And you," he added, turning on Jeff, "I thought you were my friend!"

With that, he grabbed his gear and stormed away from the field, leaving Jeff and Todd staring at each other in disbelief.

3

Garry avoided Todd and Jeff for the rest of the afternoon. At dinner, he made himself a sandwich and snuck out of the mess hall with it rather than sit with his teammates. And that night, he jammed his new earplugs into his ears and pretended to be asleep when the others called for him to join their campfire.

He must have really fallen asleep, though, for the next thing he knew it was morning. He sat up, feeling completely rested — and completely foolish for the way he'd acted the night before. He found his brother and

Jeff at breakfast and slid onto the bench next to them.

"Um, hey there," he mumbled. "Sorry about —"

Todd held up a hand. "'Nuff said. I've been there, remember? Just eat your breakfast."

Garry obeyed meekly. Then he asked his brother what the team was supposed to do the rest of the day.

"We've got free time this morning," Todd replied. "And then practice after lunch. Jeff and I are going swimming. Want to come?"

Garry did, so the three hit the lake after breakfast along with several of their teammates. Garry was happy to see that Michael was not among them. By the time practice rolled around, he was determined not to let the other boy get under his skin again.

That proved more difficult than he had imagined, however.

Midway through practice, Coach Hasbrouck split the team into two lines for a stationary zigzag passing drill. He dumped a bucket of lacrosse balls at one end and called, "Start it up, Conor! I need to talk with the tournament director." Then he headed over to an adjacent field where a man with a clipboard waited.

Conor scooped up a ball and threw it across to Pedro. Pedro caught it and hurled it to Eric, who was standing next to Conor. Conor, meanwhile, started another ball going.

Within moments, multiple balls were zigzagging in rapid succession back and forth across the twenty-foot divide. If one ball was dropped, there was always another one right behind it.

Garry was receiving balls from Carl and throwing them across to Michael. Carl usually threw with pinpoint accuracy, but today his tosses were a little off. Garry missed one, jumped for another, and caught a third at knee level. His throw after this third catch set Michael off on yet another rant.

"Wallis, I'd need a trampoline to catch that!" he yelled as the ball sailed far above his head. "You see a trampoline here? No? Then how about you aim for my stick instead of the clouds!"

A few nearby Rockets tittered. Evan, standing next to Michael as usual, held up his hand for a high five. Michael, as usual, ignored him, instead focusing his attention — and sarcasm — on Garry.

"My stick doesn't telescope eight feet in the air, you know! Or do you think I can bring the ball down to earth with the power of my mind?"

Garry was about to retort that he didn't think Michael could do *anything* with the power of his mind when — *thwap!* A fast-moving ball struck his side.

"Sorry, Garry," Carl called apologetically. "I thought you were ready!"

"Oh, he's ready all right," Michael said with a snort. "Ready to ride the pine in the game tomorrow, I'd say!"

Any intention Garry had of putting up with Michael's taunts went straight out the window then. "Shut your yap, Donofrio! Wait, never mind. I'll shut it for you!"

Blood boiling, he scooped up the ball that had hit him and flung it as hard as he could at Michael. Michael ducked. The ball bounced away into the tall grass.

"Ooooo," Evan said. "You gonna stand for that, D-man?"

Michael narrowed his eyes and tapped the neck of his stick against his gloved hand. "I don't think I am, Evan."

Garry took a step toward him but was stopped by a firm hand on his shoulder.

"All right," Coach Hasbrouck said quietly. "That's enough."

Garry stiffened for a moment. Then all his anger vanished, replaced by shame. "Sorry, Coach," he mumbled.

The coach dropped his hand and nodded. "Okay." He blew a blast on his whistle. "Set up for the run-and-pass drill. Two lines midfield, ball in the right line. Let's see some hustle and some teamwork!"

Garry hurried to the left sideline. Jeff and Todd came up behind him.

"Man, why do you bother mixing it up with Donofrio?" Todd said in a low voice.

"The guy's a pile of dog doo," Jeff added. "And you know what happens when you mess around with dog doo? You end up smelling just like it, that's what!"

Garry swished his stick head through the grass. "I know, I know. I'll try to ignore him."

"Good," Todd agreed. Then he looked over to the other line and gave Garry a shove. "But don't start now, because he's your partner for the drill and it's your turn!"

Michael had already started down the field. Garry had to pour on the speed to draw level with him. When he did, Michael fired such a hard pass that the ball nearly tore the stick out of Garry's hand.

But at least I caught it, Garry thought grimly. *Bet "D-man" didn't expect that!*

4

Garry and Michael tossed the ball back and forth the rest of the way down the field. Garry ended up with it close to the goal and rocketed a shot into the net. Then he retrieved the ball and returned to the end of his line. To his relief, he had a different partner the next time around.

After fifteen minutes, the coach called them together. "Another team is taking over the field soon. What do you say to a little six-on-six scrimmage in the time we have left?"

The Rockets were all in favor, so Coach Hasbrouck split them into two teams. Garry had Todd, Conor, Brandon, Pedro, and Andrew on his side; playing against them were Michael, Jeff, Carl, Evan, Eric, and Samuel. Christopher, the team's starting goalkeeper, volunteered to referee with the coach.

Garry headed to the center X for the face-off. Michael stood opposite him. He gave Garry a lazy grin.

"Well, this is going to be a piece of cake," he drawled. "Even if you do get the ball before me, you'll drop it, like you've been dropping balls all practice!"

Garry flushed a deep red. He had a sarcastic retort on the tip of his tongue, but then he remembered what Jeff had said about dog doo. So as difficult as it was, he kept his mouth shut.

The coach appeared then and put the ball on the ground between the two boys. "Ready?"

Garry put in his mouth guard and squatted

down. He held his stick parallel to and almost touching the ground, right hand near the throat, left hand midway down the shaft. His muscles tensed with anticipation. "Ready, Coach," he answered.

Michael crouched down too, and grunted his readiness to the coach.

"At my signal, then. And make it look good," Coach Hasbrouck added with a grin. "The next team is here already. Let's show them what they'll be up against when they play us tomorrow!" He stepped back out of the way and gave a blast on his whistle.

Garry moved fast, but Michael moved faster. He clamped his stick over the ball and raked it backward with one swift move. The ball flew over the grass behind him and right into the pocket of Evan's stick.

Evan scooped up the ball and fed it back to Michael. Michael made a nice over-the-shoulder catch and took off down the field, stick held high and twisting in his hands to keep the ball secure in the pocket.

"Take it away!" Evan cried.

Don't mind if I do, Evan, Garry thought as he chased Michael down the field. He leveled his stick and poke-checked the shaft of the other boy's stick. The jab was just strong enough to pop the ball free — and just unexpected enough to catch Michael off guard. Garry was heading in the opposite direction with the ball before Michael could even turn around.

Evan started toward Garry but Garry whirled away and made for the sideline. He intended to streak down the line and then cut in toward the goal. But Jeff charged him, matching him step for step while trying to edge him out-of-bounds.

"Here!" Pedro called from midfield.

Garry flung the ball to him with a quick

downward slash of his stick. Pedro caught it just as Samuel reached him.

"Ball!" Samuel yelled to let his teammates know that he was covering Pedro. He shadowed the fleet-footed attackman for several yards.

But then Pedro stopped short. Samuel took a few steps more before realizing his man was no longer next to him. Pedro, meanwhile, found Conor cutting across the field.

Conor snagged the ball out of the air. He and Pedro switched places so that he was now carrying the ball down the middle of the field.

Garry ran parallel to his teammates. When Conor got into trouble, he was ready to receive his pass.

But Eric, playing defense, guessed that Conor would feed the ball to Garry. He slid in front of Garry just as Conor threw. *Fwap!*

The ball stuck in Eric's pocket instead of Garry's, and suddenly the tide had turned again.

Eric hurled the ball to Jeff, who relayed it to Michael.

"Back!" Jeff yelled, looking for a return pass.

But Michael held it instead of passing. He dodged and feinted his way around two defenders, including Todd, and fired the ball into the empty net.

"Oh, yeah!" Evan bellowed.

Michael raised a hand to acknowledge the praise, and then pretended to lick his finger and make a tally mark in the air. "One for the good guys," he said as he strode to the center X.

Garry bit his lip to keep from remarking about how easy it was to score when there wasn't a goalie to block the shot. *Let your moves do the talking for you,* he told himself as he squatted for the face-off.

Christopher put the ball between them, then trotted back out of the way and yelled, "Game on!"

This time, Garry's stick covered the ball before Michael's did. With a practiced flick, he sent the ball bouncing across the grass to Pedro. Pedro scooped it up and made a dash for the goal.

Once more, Samuel challenged him. He mirrored Pedro the length of the field, positioning himself between the attackman and the goal.

Pedro saw he didn't have a clean shot. He couldn't find an open man to pass to either, so he kept moving until he was behind the goal.

Garry hurried to the top of the crease, in case Pedro came around the other side of the goal. Todd was several steps behind him, with Michael defending him.

Conor, meanwhile, raced down to take up position behind the goal with Pedro. "Pick!" he said urgently as he ran by the Wallis brothers.

Garry glanced at Todd to see if he'd heard Conor. Todd was cutting to the left of the goal, Michael at his side. Garry grinned. His brother had heard, all right!

The pick was one of Garry's favorite plays. While Conor and Pedro played keep-away from Samuel with the ball behind the net, he darted back and forth in front of the goal, stick up as if he were waiting for a pass. Jeff matched his every step. Todd, mean-while, was dancing around as if trying to elude Michael.

Then suddenly, Garry hit the brakes, back-pedaled away from Jeff, and planted himself near Todd.

At the same time, Todd rushed toward his brother. Michael followed, watching Todd intently.

Blam! Michael ran smack into Garry! The blow nearly knocked Garry off his feet, but that was the price one paid when setting a successful pick.

Now free of his defender, Todd raced on, caught the throw from Conor, and rocketed the ball into the net.

Garry whooped and ran to give his brother a jumping high five.

Michael pounded his stick into the ground and snarled, "Enjoy it now, Wallises. It's the last time either of you will touch the ball this afternoon!"

5

Michael backed up his threat by winning the third face-off. But his team didn't have possession for long because Carl missed the scoop, giving Andrew time to dash forward and nab the ball out of the grass.

"Go for it!" Garry yelled.

Andrew threw over to Brandon. Brandon relayed it to Todd. Todd ran with the ball for several feet and then sent it downfield toward Pedro . . .

. . . who didn't get it because Samuel stole

it, turned on a dime, and flashed it back the other way to Eric. Then Samuel, Eric, and Evan thundered down the field, passing back and forth, with Michael, Jeff, and Carl racing along in front of them.

"Pass it up already, will you?" Michael yelled.

Eric obeyed — only to see Todd leap up and slap the ball down to the ground.

"Whoo-hooo!" Garry whooped, marveling at how much his brother had improved since spring.

Todd scooped up the ball and threw to him. Garry made a clean catch and started down the field. Pedro, running parallel and just a bit ahead, signaled for a pass. Garry fired the ball to him.

Wham! Moments after the ball left his stick someone slammed into him from behind, knocking him to the ground!

Tweet! The sharp whistle brought play to a halt.

"What're you doing?" Coach Hasbrouck bellowed. "This is lacrosse, not football!"

Garry rolled over, spat out his mouth guard, and sat up, dazed. "What happened?"

"Your teammate pretty much tackled you, that's what happened," an unfamiliar voice answered.

Garry turned to see a small, wiry boy on the sidelines. "Which teammate?" he asked.

"The one your coach is heading to."

Garry looked to where the boy was pointing. "Michael. Of course."

The other boy was smirking at Garry. But the smirk vanished the moment Coach Hasbrouck appeared at his side, replaced by a look of concern.

Garry stood up just as Coach Hasbrouck and Michael came over.

"Wallis, you okay?" Michael asked in a

worried tone — a tone Garry wasn't buying for a minute.

"Yeah, I'm fine, no thanks to you!" he fumed.

Now Michael put on a hurt face. "You don't think I hit you on purpose, do you?" He turned to Coach Hasbrouck. "I'm telling you, I tripped over something while I was chasing Wallis down the line."

Evan appeared at Michael's side. "He did, Coach, I saw him!" He made a big show of shaking his head. "I think there must be a bump in the field, or maybe a gopher hole, or even a rock! Michael's lucky he didn't get hurt!"

"Anyway," Michael said, ignoring Evan, "no harm done, right, Wallis?"

Garry gave him a long look. "Right, Donofrio," he said at last.

Just then, a man wearing a shirt with the team name THUNDER emblazoned across

35

the chest tapped Coach Hasbrouck on the shoulder. "You about through here? It's my team's turn on the field."

The coach sighed and nodded. "We'll get out of your way. Have a good practice."

Garry headed to the sidelines to gather his belongings. The wiry boy who'd pointed out Michael drew alongside him.

"Listen, I thought you should know that your teammate didn't trip," he said in a low voice. "He shoved you on purpose."

Garry kicked at the grass. He knew Michael had deliberately pushed him, but he'd hoped no one else did. He hated the fact that someone else — a member of the competition, no less! — had witnessed it. He felt his face turn red and yanked his sweatshirt on over his head to cover his embarrassment.

"Um, you know you're bleeding, right?" The kid pointed to Garry's knee.

Garry peered down and groaned. Sure enough, a gash there was oozing blood. "Figures," he mumbled.

"Here." The boy dug around in his own equipment bag, pulled out a small first aid kit, and handed it to Garry. "Don't ask," he said at Garry's look. "My mom makes me keep it in there." He put out his hand. "I'm Scottie. Who are you?"

Garry shook Scottie's hand and told him his name. "I'm an attackman for the Rockets," he added.

Scottie grinned. "Guess I'll have to be on the lookout for you. I play goalkeeper for the Thunder." He looked over his shoulder. "My practice is starting. See you around, Garry."

"What should I do with this?" Garry held up the first aid kit.

Scottie made a face. "Leave it on the bench. If I'm lucky, someone will take it!"

Garry laughed as Scottie jogged onto the field. Then he peeled open the bandage, stuck it on his knee, and tucked the wrapper into his sweatshirt pocket.

He seems like a nice kid. Wonder if he's any good in goal?

Curious, he watched the Thunder practice for a few minutes, long enough to see that Scottie wasn't good — he was awesome.

It's going to be tough getting the ball past him! Garry thought.

6

Hey, Garry!"

Garry turned to see Jeff waving to him. "Todd, Conor, and I are going to shower up and then play cards until dinner. Want to come?"

Garry was about to say no. Then he remembered how lousy he'd felt the night before, when he'd sat alone in the cabin instead of doing fun stuff with the others. So he nodded, picked up his duffel bag, and followed Jeff. After quick showers, they played several games of rummy 500, crazy eights, and penny poker. Then the dinner bell rang.

"At last!" Garry said. "I'm starving!"

The hall was already crowded with boys in line to pick up their meals. There were eight teams participating in the tournament and while each team slept in a separate section of the camp — the Rockets' section was called Boulders, so named for the huge rocks that studded the deep woods behind their cabins — all the players ate together.

"Hot dogs, french fries, and applesauce," Todd announced as he craned his neck to see what was being served. "And they've got the soup, sandwich, and salad bar too. That's where I'm headed."

The sandwich bar had all kinds of breads, meats, and cheeses. It also had tuna, chopped hard-boiled eggs, and different sorts of vegetables for salad. For soup there was New England clam chowder or chicken noodle.

Garry tied his sweatshirt around his waist,

grabbed a tray, plastic plate, and silverware, and followed his brother. He filled a submarine roll with sliced turkey, pickles, lettuce, and mayonnaise and then added a huge handful of potato chips and a dish of applesauce to his tray. At the drink counter, he selected a very full glass of lemonade.

Eyes on his glass, he stepped back from the counter. As he did, his foot struck something. He stumbled. His tray flew out of his hands and landed on the floor with a loud crash. As he fell, lemonade, applesauce, turkey, and chips splattered all around him.

He sat in the middle of the mess, stunned. Then he heard laughter. Everyone in the cafeteria had seen what had happened and was cracking up!

"You sure are having trouble staying upright today, Wallis!" a voice drawled.

It was Michael. He grinned wickedly and

then, with a very deliberate motion, lifted his foot and wiggled it. "Hmm, I wonder what you tripped over?"

Fury raged through Garry. He balled his hands into fists and jumped up — only to slip in his applesauce and fall again.

Michael doubled over with laughter. Evan, at Michael's side as always, slapped his knees and roared gleefully. Other nearby boys were laughing, too.

Garry wanted to die. Then he saw a hand reach down for him. He looked up, expecting to see his brother. But the hand belonged to Scottie.

"Come on, Garry," the goalkeeper urged. "Let's get out of here."

Jeff and Todd appeared then and started to clean up the mess. "Go on, Garry," his brother said. "We've got this!"

So Garry stood up and, with Scottie clearing a path in front of him, hurried through the crowd and outside. Then Scottie looked back over his shoulder.

"My coach is signaling to me," he said. "Hang on, I'll be right back."

Garry knew he should be grateful for Scottie's help. But all he wanted was to be far away from everyone. So the minute Scottie went back inside, he took off. Boys he passed looked at him strangely, but he kept running, past his cabin and onto a trail that led into the woods behind it.

The wide path quickly shrank to a scraggly dirt line barely visible in the thick brush. Garry slowed to a walk, breathing hard from the run and from anger.

I hate Michael! he fumed as he moved deeper into the forest. It was cool beneath the trees. He pulled his sweatshirt from around his waist, tugged it over his head, and kept walking. He spied a giant boulder and started toward it, kicking at roots and rocks as he went.

Then suddenly, *twang!* His foot hit something metal. It was an overturned rusty bucket half buried in the dirt. He kicked it again and then again, venting his fury with each blow.

One particularly vicious kick wrenched the bucket free of the ground. It bounced away with a clang. Garry was about to follow it when he saw something in the dirt where the bucket had been. He bent down to examine the object more closely.

It was a small cardboard matchbox. The outside of the box was decorated with fish outlines and red-and-blue curlicues. SEAFOOD EMPORIUM! was emblazoned across the top. Along one side was a rough strike plate for lighting the matches.

Garry picked it up and slid open the tiny

drawer. Inside were six wooden matches. He dumped them into his hand, expecting them to feel damp. But, having been protected by the bucket, they and the box were bone-dry.

He stared at them for a long minute — and found himself suddenly itching to light one and watch it burn.

If only there was someplace safe to do it, he thought.

Then he had an idea. He put the matches back in the box, shoved the box into his sweatshirt pocket, and climbed the boulder. When he got to the top, he looked and listened to make sure he was alone. The woods were empty and the only sounds were the wind in the trees and the rushing water of a nearby river.

He took the box out of his pocket, removed a match, and scraped the head against the strike plate.

Fssss! The match caught fire instantly. Garry was so surprised that he dropped it.

Fortunately, there was nothing on the boulder that could burn, which was why Garry had chosen to light the match atop it in the first place. He watched in fascination as the flame licked down the length of the matchstick. That tiny bit of fire echoed the blaze of fury in his gut — and when the match burned out, his own angry fire began to fizzle out too.

He took out a second match and did it again. A sudden breeze blew that one out before he could put it on the boulder. So he tried to light a third. But the strike plate had worn off by then and the match didn't catch.

I need something rough to strike the match head against, Garry thought.

The surface beneath him was too bumpy and he was certain the match would snap in half if he tried to light it there. But near the edge where he'd climbed up there was a flat place that he thought would do. He put the box in his sweatshirt pocket and carried the match over to the spot.

He scraped it against the boulder's surface. The match caught right away. Garry held it up and watched it burn toward his fingers.

"Garry, wait!"

The shout cut through the stillness of the forest. Startled, Garry dropped the match and jumped up.

"Who's there?"

The only reply was the sharp *crack* of a branch snapping in two.

Then —

"Help! Help! Garry, help me!"

7

Garry gasped. The cry had come from the direction of the river! He leaped from the boulder and ran toward the sound. Branches lashed against his face. A thick root grabbed his sneakers and — "Ooof!" — he stumbled and sprawled face-first in the dirt. A long blaze of dirt streaked his sweatshirt but he barely noticed. He was up and crashing through a thicket and onto the riverbank.

"Is there someone out there?" he yelled.

"Over here!"

Garry turned in the direction of the voice — and sucked in his breath. Clinging to a jagged rock in the middle of the churning rapids was Scottie!

"Oh, my gosh! Hold on! I'm coming!" Garry started to step onto a rock in the river.

"No! Stay back! That's how I fell —!" A foaming wave engulfed the boy's head, cutting off his cry.

"Okay, okay!" Garry looked around desperately. Rocks, leaves, bushes — they were no help! Then he spotted a long tree branch stuck in the mud farther up the bank.

"I've got it!" he cried. He raced up the river edge, yanked until the branch pulled free, and dragged it back. Then he sat down on the muddy bank, braced his feet against two big rocks so he wouldn't slip forward, and yelled, "Here it comes!"

He swooped the tree limb over the rushing water, praying that it would reach Scottie. It did.

"Got it?" he yelled. Scottie didn't answer,

and for one heart-stopping moment Garry thought he'd struck him on the head or swept him from the rock with the leafy limb.

Then the branch vibrated in his hands and he guessed that Scottie had grabbed it.

"Okay, I'm going to pull you in now, so hold on tight!"

He took a deep breath and then, hand over hand, slowly pulled the branch and the boy toward him. His backside sank deep into the cold mud, his palms were scraped by the rough bark, and his arms and legs ached from fighting the current and pulling the branch. But at last, he dragged Scottie to safety.

"Th-thanks!" Scottie sputtered. "I thought I was a g-g-goner!" A cool breeze had set the wet boy's teeth chattering. Garry took off his sweatshirt and gave it to him.

Scottie put it on, pulled his knees to his chest, and wrapped his arms around them.

After a moment, he stopped shivering. Then he gave Garry a puzzled look. "How did you get to me so quickly?"

Garry blinked at the question. "I ran when I heard you yell. Scottie, what are you doing out here?"

Scottie hugged his knees closer. "I was looking for you!"

"Why?"

Scottie didn't answer right away. Then he said, "I wanted to make sure you were okay. See, I've been in your position before. I was bullied by a big jerk last year, kind of like Donofrio's bullying you."

"Michael's not bullying me!" Garry protested. "I mean, sure, he calls me names, makes fun of me when I mess up on the field, slams me to the ground on purpose, trips me . . ." His voice trailed away.

Scottie gave a small shrug. "That sure sounds like bullying to me."

Garry picked up a rock and threw it into the river. "Yeah, maybe you're right. But don't worry about me, I can handle Michael. I have before, anyway."

"You have?" Scottie looked at him with interest. "How?"

Garry told him what had happened between Michael and Todd and how he had dealt with it.

Scottie whistled in admiration. "You kept him from being top scorer? Cool."

"Yeah, well, he's paying me back now. So what's your story? Why were you being bullied?"

Scottie held up his arms. The sleeves of Garry's sweatshirt covered his hands. "In case you hadn't noticed, I'm not a big guy."

"So?"

"So even though I'm small, I've got great reflexes and can read the action on the field better than anyone else on my team."

Garry raised his eyebrows.

Scottie laughed. "I know it sounds like I'm bragging, but really, it's the truth."

Garry smiled. "Yeah, I know. I watched you during practice earlier."

"Anyway," Scottie continued, "last year, another kid, someone bigger and older than me, wanted to be starting goalkeeper. But I got the position instead of him. He, um, didn't like that too much. To say the least."

"What'd he do to you?"

Scottie didn't answer right away. Instead, he took off his wet sneakers and dug his toes into the slick mud. "Oh, the usual stuff," he said finally. "Teasing, throwing my hat around on the school bus, getting other kids to call me Snottie. I shouldn't have let it get to me, but it did, you know?"

Garry nodded. He knew.

"Anyway, life is much better now," Scottie said.

"Because you stood up to him?"

Scottie flashed a mischievous grin. "Because he moved up a division this year so we're not on the same team anymore!"

Garry grinned too. Then he stood up and twisted around to look at his muddy backside. "I gotta change. Want to get going?"

Scottie ran his fingers through his wet hair. "Good idea. My head's freezing." He put his shoes back on and stood too. Then he reached behind his neck for something. "Hey," he said when he came up empty-handed, "how come your sweatshirt doesn't have a hood?"

"My brother and I kept getting our sweatshirts mixed up, so I cut the hood off mine. I never liked the way it felt, anyway."

They walked along the trail out of the woods in silence for a few minutes. Then Scottie remarked, "You know they give out the top scorer award after this tournament, don't you?"

"Yeah, I'm sure good ol' Michael will be trying for it."

Scottie waggled his eyebrows. "Well, he won't get any help from me, I can tell you that!" Then he laughed. "You know what would be really great? If you won it instead of him!"

Garry smiled. "It'd be a real kick in his ego, that's for sure!"

The sun was going down when they reached the edge of the woods. Scottie started to take off the sweatshirt but Garry waved him off. "Keep it for now. You need it more than I do."

The two boys parted company and Garry hurried back to his cabin. He was changing out of his muddy shorts when Todd and Jeff came in.

Todd flopped onto his bunk. "What happened to you?"

Jeff eyed Garry's filthy shorts and sneakers. "Mud wrestling, from the looks of it!" he said with a laugh.

"Ha-ha," Garry said.

"Seriously, we've been looking all over for you," Todd said. "So where —"

Todd was cut off by the crackle of the loudspeaker. "Attention, attention!" came an urgent voice. "There is a fire in the woods behind the Boulders section of camp! The fire department is on the way but we still need everyone to report immediately to the lake for the bucket brigade!"

8

For one long second, Garry, Jeff, and Todd stared at one another.

"Holy cow!" Todd finally cried. "Come on!"

They jumped up and ran from the cabin.

Garry smelled the smoke the moment he set foot outside. He craned his neck around and looked up. A black plume blocked out the stars that had begun to emerge in the night sky. Garry traced the smoke trail down to the treetops, knowing the fire had to be just below. Then he dropped his gaze lower — and found himself staring at the path he had followed into the woods.

His mouth turned dry. *That path leads to the boulder where I was lighting matches.*

"Come on, Garry, we gotta go help!" Todd yelled.

Garry took a few faltering steps backward, then turned and raced after his brother. His mind was racing even faster than his feet, asking the same question over and over.

Did I start the fire?

His breathing was ragged when he reached the lake. Four lines of boys and men had already been formed. Buckets of water and sand were being passed hand to hand down the line and into the woods to the fire. Empty buckets were returning down other lines. Jeff and Todd immediately joined a line to help.

Garry did too, but his mind wasn't on the work. It was replaying the scene on the boulder in his mind.

The first match burned out. The second match blew out. The third match . . .

He nearly let go of the bucket of sand he was holding.

I dropped the third match when I heard Scottie yell! I don't know if it burned out or not! And if it didn't . . .

If it didn't, it could very well have caused the fire. Meaning *he* had caused the fire.

"Come on, kid, hurry it up with that bucket!" the boy next to Garry urged. "We've got to get this fire out!"

A fire you started, a voice inside his head accused.

I don't know that for sure! he argued with himself. *There could have been someone else out there!*

Someone else *was* out there, he suddenly realized. Scottie!

Of course, the Thunder goalkeeper hadn't

started the blaze — unless he'd lit the fire and then jumped in the freezing cold river.

Freezing cold . . . Garry's heart started hammering in his chest.

Scottie has my sweatshirt! The matches are still inside the pocket. What if he finds them — and puts two and two together?

Garry looked up and down the line, searching for Scottie. He didn't find him. There was nothing to do then but continue passing buckets.

After what seemed like an eternity, a call came down the line that the fire department had arrived and put out the last of the flames. Now the boys were all to go to the mess hall.

As the crowd began moving, Garry searched for Scottie again. This time, he found him. He ran toward his new friend — but then stopped short. Scottie had changed out of his wet clothes and was no longer wearing the Rockets sweatshirt.

Scottie waved and hurried over. "Wow, can you believe this?" he said as they climbed the wooden stairs into the mess hall. "Do you think that fire was anywhere near where we were?"

Garry blinked, suddenly hopeful. *Maybe Scottie didn't find the matches after all! If he did, wouldn't he have asked about them?*

But in the next moment, his heart sank down to his toes.

"Say, Garry," Scottie said, his voice low, "are you going to tell someone what happened out there? Because if you don't, I will."

Garry sank down onto a bench. "Wha — what do you mean?"

"I mean, someone should know what you did! You should at least tell your coach."

Garry hung his head. "But I don't know for sure that I did it!"

"Huh?" Scottie gave him a surprised look. "Of course you did it! No one else was —"

Whatever Scottie was going to say got cut off by a shout from one of his teammates. "Whoops, I gotta go sit with my team. But listen, tell your coach — or I will!" With that, he hurried to join the rest of the Thunder, leaving Garry to stare after him in dismay.

Jeff appeared at that moment. "Who's that kid?" he asked. "And what does he want you to tell my dad?"

arry was saved from answering by the crackle of a microphone. He turned in his seat to face the stage at the far end of the mess hall. There stood a burly man in a fire-fighter's uniform.

"Your attention, please, boys," he said. "The fire that started behind the Boulders section is out. And I want to take a moment to point out the boy responsible for that."

For one horrid second, Garry thought the firefighter was talking about him. But then the man called out a different name:

"Michael Donofrio, will you come here, please?"

Every head swiveled. Usually, Michael's walk was a casual saunter, as if he had all the time in the world. This time, it was a pure strut.

The fire chief laid a hand on Michael's shoulder. "When this young man saw the smoke, he dialed 9-1-1. Thanks to him, what could have been a major forest fire was just a small blaze. Well done, son."

Michael puffed out his chest. "Just being a responsible citizen, sir."

"There's a first time for everything," Jeff whispered as applause echoed through the room.

Todd pointed at the stage. "Oh, no!" He started choking with laughter. "I — I think he's going to give a speech!"

Sure enough, Michael was holding up his

hands for silence. "Men," he said when everyone's eyes were upon him, "I hope this won't make any of you treat me any differently. Of course," he added, "if it weren't for me, the tournament would probably be canceled because everything would be burned to the ground!" He put a hand on his heart. "But I'm still the same guy you've always known."

"Too bad," Todd commented to Jeff's amusement.

The firefighter took back the microphone. "I have one other announcement. We are launching an investigation into the cause of the fire. Anyone who has any information should contact us, your coaches, or the tournament director immediately." He paused, as if waiting for someone to step forward.

At that moment, Garry saw Scottie staring at him. His heart started to thump furiously. Would Scottie stand and tell everyone that he had found matches in Garry's sweatshirt pocket?

But Scottie stayed in his seat, only rising when the fire chief dismissed them to their cabins. Garry tried to find him in the crowd. But the goalkeeper had disappeared.

10

Sleep didn't come easily to Garry that night.

It's all Michael's fault, he thought as he tossed and turned. *That fire wouldn't have started if he hadn't humiliated me in the mess hall! Scottie shares the blame too. If he hadn't yelled, I wouldn't have dropped that match!*

But even as these thoughts raced through his mind, he knew they weren't true. No one had forced him to light those matches. He had done that, even though he knew it wasn't a good idea.

That's when he knew what he had to do. He had to confess.

He rolled over and checked his watch. It was after midnight, too late to go to the coach.

I'll tell him everything first thing in the morning. I'll probably get booted out of the tournament, maybe even off the team, but that's no one's fault but my own.

Then he rolled back over and finally fell into a deep slumber. In fact, he slept so soundly that he didn't wake until the break-fast bell sounded. Groggy, he stumbled out of his bunk, changed into shorts and a T-shirt, and hurried to the mess hall, intending to find Coach Hasbrouck and tell him what happened.

Unfortunately, the coach was sitting at a table with all the other coaches. From the expressions on their faces, they seemed to be having a very serious discussion. One look at them, and Garry lost his nerve.

After breakfast, he told himself.

But when the meal ended, there wasn't time to talk to the coach, because the Rockets were playing in the first game of the day. Garry had no choice but to hurry back to his cabin, get into uniform, and report to the field with his brother and Jeff.

I have to put the fire and Scottie out of my mind, he thought.

But that wasn't going to be easy. The Rockets were playing the Thunder — which meant he was going to be facing Scottie all morning!

Sure enough, as he passed by the Thunders bench, he saw Scottie. The goalkeeper was sitting with his head bowed, his arms resting on his legs. Garry wanted to tell him that he intended to tell his coach what had happened. But then Scottie looked up and gave him a blank stare. Once again, Garry lost his nerve.

"Okay, Rockets, onto the field for warm-ups!" Coach Hasbrouck called.

After their running and stretching exercises, it was time to play. As usual, Garry, Michael, and Conor made up the attacking lineup. Behind them were middies Evan, Jeff, and Samuel. Carl, Eric, and Brandon were on defense, with Christopher in the goal. Todd, Pedro, and Andrew sat on the bench, ready to bring fresh energy to the field when needed.

Garry bounced on his toes in the wing area as the Thunder players took up their positions for the face-off. Opposite Michael at the center X was a ferocious-looking Thunder attacker.

The referee placed the ball between the two, stepped back, and blew his whistle.

Michael instantly flipped his stick head over the ball and raked the rubber sphere between his legs. The Thunder attacker tried to dig it free but Michael scooped it up and twisted away to begin a run down the field.

Garry exploded out of the wing area to race parallel with Michael. He called for a pass, but Michael seemed determined to make this first goal attempt a one-man show. He dodged, feinted, and twirled down the field, cradling the ball up high.

Then he got in trouble. A defenseman leaped out and poke-checked the shaft of his stick. Some players would have lost the ball then, but not Michael. When the jab popped the ball free, he swooped his stick down, pocket opening skyward, and reclaimed it! Two steps more and he was just outside the crease.

Garry ran forward to offer backup just as Scottie came out of the goal to face Michael.

Swish! Down came Michael's stick.

Zoom! The ball streaked on a line toward the net. Then —

Thwap! Scottie lunged sideways and nabbed it!

The amazing save left Michael staring dumbfounded for more than a second. By the time he recovered his wits, the ball was halfway down the field. Two minutes later, the Thunder had pushed it past Christopher and into the goal.

Garry knew he should be disappointed that Michael hadn't scored, but he couldn't help feeling his teammate had gotten what he deserved. Lacrosse was a team sport, after all. Maybe if Michael had passed the ball to Garry or another Rocket, the score would be Rockets 1, Thunder 0, instead of the other way around.

Besides, Scottie deserved credit for the spectacular save. And it wasn't the only one he made the first quarter. By the time fifteen minutes had passed, he had only let three balls past him into the net. Garry had thrown one of those balls, Conor another, and Jeff had sent in the third after receiving an unexpected pass from Evan.

Unfortunately for the Rockets, the Thunder had chalked up five goals during that same quarter. During the short break, Coach Hasbrouck took Christopher aside and spoke to him in a low voice. Whatever the coach had said seemed to make a difference, for in the second quarter, the Rockets goalkeeper allowed the Thunder to score only two goals. The Rockets, meanwhile, slashed in four to tie things up, with Garry scoring two and Jeff and Michael one each.

Garry was surprised. He had always contributed his share of goals, but it was usually Michael who netted the most per game. But he now had four and Michael only one! He couldn't help wonder what was making the difference.

Michael, it turned out, had been wondering the same thing — and he let Garry know what he thought.

"Your buddy in the goal sure seems to be giving you a break," he growled.

Garry's jaw dropped. "You think Scottie is *letting* me score?"

Michael snorted. "You got another answer for why he's stopping everything I send — and missing all your shots?"

And unfortunately, Garry didn't.

Unless it's his way of repaying me for pulling him from the river?

11

Coach Hasbrouck clapped his hands, calling Garry and the rest of the team to attention. He praised them for pulling into the lead but then pointed out that there was still a whole half to go.

"You're playing well, don't get me wrong," he said. "But they have plenty of time to surge ahead. And in case you hadn't noticed, their goalie is outstanding. To get the ball past him, you'll have to be one step ahead of him. You won't be able to just carry it downfield and put it in the net" — here he looked pointedly at Michael — "you'll need to work it around until there's an opening."

He knelt down and laid a dry-erase board in the grass in front of him. "Right, here's a play I want you to try. It's called the middie sweep. It starts with the ball with the right middie." He glanced up. "Todd, that's you this quarter. You're subbing in for Samuel."

Todd nodded.

"Michael, you take up position at the top of the crease, here." Coach Hasbrouck marked a spot outside the goal circle. Then he drew in two other spots behind the goal. "Garry and Conor, you hustle behind and start switching off. You're there to distract the goalie and to be backup shooters, if necessary. So keep your eyes on the action."

Now the coach marked another spot in front of the goal but behind Michael's position. "Jeff, you stack up behind Michael, here. Evan, you're parallel to Jeff on the left side. Everyone got it?"

When the players nodded, the coach gestured to Todd. "Todd, when you see that these five are in their places, you bring the ball across the line. Fire it over to Jeff." He drew a sharp arrow from Todd's mark to Jeff's. "Then cut across the field between Jeff and Michael" — a dashed line indicated the path — "and take a return pass from Jeff. Use Michael as a screen and take a shot on goal if you can."

Michael made a disgusted sound in his throat.

Coach Hasbrouck looked up sharply. "You have a question, Donofrio?"

"No. Sir," Michael replied with exaggerated politeness.

The coach pressed his lips together in a

thin line. Then he continued. "Jeff, after you pass to Todd, dodge around your defender to Michael's other side. If Todd gets in trouble, he'll look for you. Then *you'll* use Michael to screen *your* shot. Meanwhile, Evan, you fall back on defense."

"What about us, Coach?" Conor asked.

"You two stay behind the goal and keep moving. Remember, Todd or Jeff might need you as backup. Everyone got it?"

The team nodded as one just as the buzzer signaled the end of the break.

The coach stood. "Michael, rake the ball back to Todd if you win the face-off. Todd, call for the middie sweep. I think the play just might confuse that hotshot goalie, so work it when you can. Okay, hands in the middle. Go, Rockets!"

The players echoed the cry. Garry bumped fists with his brother.

"Make it work, bro," he said.

"I will, if Michael lets me!" Todd replied grimly.

Garry hustled to the wing area and Todd to his midfield position for the face-off.

Tweet! The referee blew his whistle.

Michael stabbed at the ball and controlled it. But he didn't pass off to Todd as the coach had instructed.

"Come on, Donofrio, give it up!" Garry cried as Michael tore down the field with the ball in his stick pocket.

Michael ignored him. Two defenders bounded toward him. One leveled his stick at him to poke-check the ball free.

Michael whirled away from one and feinted around the other.

"Here!" Todd cried.

This time Michael did pass. Todd caught it cleanly.

"Back!" Michael held his stick high for a return pass.

Todd ignored him. "Middie sweep!" he cried.

The Rockets moved like clockwork. Todd cradled the ball safely in his pocket and hurried down the sideline. Garry streaked past Scottie and took up his position behind the goal. Conor reached his spot at the same time. Evan and Jeff moved into position too.

Now the only person not in the right place was Michael. Then he seemed to realize that since he didn't have the ball, he had no choice but to take part in the play.

Todd set the middie sweep in motion. He whipped the ball to Jeff and cut across in front of Michael. Jeff sent the ball back to him. Todd spun to look for the shot.

But Scottie had followed his movements and filled the empty corner of the net.

So Todd rocketed the ball back to Jeff. Jeff nabbed it only to have a Thunder defender bulldoze a shoulder into his ribs. Jeff stumbled and the ball bounced to the ground. He and the Thunder defender stabbed their stick heads at it.

But then Michael joined the fight. He captured the ball, twisted around, and slashed his stick sideways in a vicious and off-balance shot.

The ball flew toward an empty corner of the net, a surefire goal — if the corner had stayed empty, that is.

Stick outstretched, Scottie hurtled across the goal mouth and snared the ball just before it crossed inside. The ball didn't stay in his oversize pocket for long, however. As Scottie made the save, one of his middies moved to collect the outlet pass. Scottie flicked the ball to him in a move so perfectly executed that it was obvious the two players had done the same thing many times before.

Michael, meanwhile, had been so certain of the goal that he had raised his stick in victory. For the second time that game, he stood rooted to the spot, jaw slack with amazement.

12

Any other time, Garry would have paused to enjoy Michael's distress. But not this time.

"Fast break!" Garry heard Christopher yell from the Rockets goal.

Brandon came out to challenge the Thunder player carrying the ball. Quick as a wink, the attacker flung the ball to his teammate, who in turn hurled it right back as Brandon followed the throw.

With Brandon pulled out of position, the first attacker switched to a one-handed cradle and held up his free arm to fend off Brandon's approach.

"Hold!" Christopher yelled from the Rockets goal, signaling for Brandon to try to force the attacker toward the sideline and away from the crease.

Brandon did his best, edging as close as he could to the attacker. But the Thunder player wasn't intimidated. He whirled away, switched to a two-handed cradle, and then fed the ball to his waiting teammate.

The Thunder receiver bobbled the catch! As the ball bounced away, Eric swooped in and scooped it up. He found Conor in the outlet slot and sent the ball sailing toward him.

Conor caught it cleanly and looked ready to carry it down the field. Instead, in a move rehearsed many times in practices, he fed the ball to Garry who had come charging toward the middle of the field to receive it.

Unfortunately for Conor, an enormous Thunder middie seemed to think he still had the ball. *Slam!* He hit Conor with a power-ful body check — so powerful, in fact, that Conor's feet left the ground on impact!

The referee immediately blew his whistle and pointed a finger at the Thunder middie. "Two-minute penalty for illegal checking!"

Garry was close enough to see the mid-fielder glowering beneath his helmet. But the Thunder player ran to the penalty box at the sidelines without protest.

"Okay, Rockets, it's a power play!" Coach Hasbrouck bellowed. "Plan A! You've got two minutes to make it happen!"

Plan A, the Rockets' primary extra man offense strategy, called for the six offensive players to circle the perimeter of the goal. Michael, Garry, Conor, Jeff, Todd, and Evan raced to their positions and began to deliver short, quick passes back and forth around the goal. Their object was to find the best angle and get off a shot or to pull the defense out of position and create a scoring opportunity for someone else.

Garry received a sharp pass from Conor, squared off as if to shoot, and then fired the ball over to Todd. Todd twisted away from a savage poke check and threw a high toss over his defender to Evan. The throw was just a bit past Evan, however, and he missed the catch.

"Pick it up!" Michael screamed. Evan stabbed at the ball and scooped it up. Michael held out his stick to receive the pass.

Instead, Evan threw to Jeff.

Jeff lunged forward, caught it, and then flipped it up and over his shoulder in a backward pass. It was a risky move, because a Thunder defender was close by.

But Garry was closer. He grabbed the ball out of the air and spun away from the defender.

"Can't see!" he heard Scottie cry.

Now's my chance! Garry swung around

the defender and flicked the ball toward the lower corner of the net.

Scottie swung his stick head at it — and missed the save!

"Woo-hoo!" Jeff cheered as the other Rockets swarmed Garry to congratulate him. Michael gave him a knowing look, but Garry ignored it. He knew for sure that his shot had caught Scottie by surprise. Maybe Scottie had let him score once or twice before, but not this time.

The rest of the second half was a hard-fought battle between the two evenly matched teams. The Rockets used the middie sweep play twice more; one of the times, Todd scored. His grin after the goal nearly split his face it was so wide.

By the game's end, the score stood at Rockets 15, Thunder 12. Garry, to his amazement, had scored seven of his team's goals, a new record for him.

Any good feelings that gave him evaporated immediately after the game, however. He felt a tap on his shoulder and turned to see Scottie standing there.

"I put your sweatshirt in your cabin," the boy said. His voice was dull and he avoided Garry's eyes.

Before Garry could reply, Todd slapped him on the shoulder, crowed, "You, bro, were on *fire!*" and then moved off to celebrate with the others.

Scottie's head jerked up. He stared at Garry for a long moment.

"Yeah, you were on fire all right," he said finally. Then he spun around and stalked away.

Garry swallowed hard. Then, as quickly as he could, he gathered up the rest of his gear and made his way to the cabin.

There was his sweatshirt, neatly folded on the bunk. He pulled it down, shook it open, and reached toward the pocket.

"Looking for something?"

Michael stepped out from behind Garry's bunk. He had his lacrosse stick in his hands. In the stick's webbing was a small red-and-blue object. Michael tossed the object in the air and caught it. Garry saw then what it was — and almost got sick to his stomach.

It was the box of matches.

13

How did you get those?" Garry asked, his voice a whisper of dread.

Michael laughed low in his throat. "Let's just say I found them," he answered. He came around the bunk until he was nose to nose with Garry. "I can see the headline now: Hero Saves Camp from Fire, Names Arsonist."

Garry blanched. "Arsonist? I didn't start the fire . . . not on purpose, anyway!"

Michael smiled. "But you admit you started the fire? With these matches?"

Garry hung his head. "I-I don't know, not for sure."

"You probably did, though, right?" Michael tsked. "And yet you never said anything, not even to the coach. And now it's too late!"

Garry's head shot up. "Why? Why is it too late?" He waited for Michael to say that he'd already gone to the authorities.

Instead, Michael guffawed. "Think about it, Wallis! You'd only be confessing because I found out your secret and you're afraid I'm going to tell!"

"That's not true!" Garry protested. "I was planning to tell the coach what happened. But there wasn't time —"

"There's always time for the truth, Garry," Michael said piously. "And now I'll be the one to tell it. But first . . ."

Garry stared. "First what?"

"First, you're going to help me get something you stole from me."

"I never stole anything from you!"

"Oh, yes, you did!" Michael's eyes suddenly blazed with anger. "You stole the top scorer award from me last season! Well, now you're going to make sure I get what I deserve" — he held up the matches — "or I'll go to the coach and see that you get what you deserve!"

Garry sank down onto the bottom bunk and waited, certain Michael was going to explain — and equally certain he wasn't going to like the explanation.

"You're going to feed me the ball every time you get it," Michael said. "*Every time.* And," he continued with a nasty grin, "you'll tell everyone else on the team to do the same thing."

"Is that all?" Garry asked.

"Almost. You'll also tell your stupid brother

that he's not welcome on the Rockets. You'll get him to quit the team like I told you to do last season."

"What if I don't?"

Michael shrugged. "Then I'll tell everyone what I know. See ya." With that, he pocketed the matches and left, banging the door behind him.

Garry lay back against Conor's bunk and stared at the slats above him. He wished he could rewind time, go back to the night before, stop Michael from getting under his skin, and most of all, stop himself from lighting those matches and starting the fire.

Then suddenly, he thought of something. He sat up abruptly and almost hit his head on the bunk.

I still don't know for sure if I started that fire! Well, there's one way to find out!

He snatched up his sweatshirt and ran out of the cabin to retrace his steps back to the boulder. At one point he thought he'd gone the wrong way, but then he passed the rusty bucket that had covered the matches.

Then he saw the boulder. He blinked. There were the charred remains of a small tree and some surrounding brush, but it was several yards away from the boulder. He couldn't imagine the third match landing that far from where he'd dropped it.

Breathing hard, he scrambled to the top of the rock and found the two matches he'd lit exactly where he'd left them. Then he hurried to the spot where he'd struck the third match. He gave a cry.

There was the match, and it was only half burned!

"I didn't do it!" he crowed happily.

"Didn't do what?"

Garry jumped at the sound of the voice. He peered over the side of the boulder. It was Scottie! "What're you doing here?" he asked.

"I was about to ask you the same thing," a different voice intoned.

Garry shrank back as Coach Hasbrouck stepped into view.

"Garry, please come down from there," the coach said.

Garry hesitated, then obeyed. When he landed on the ground, he was startled to discover that Scottie's coach and the burly firefighter were with them.

"Wha-what's up?" he asked in a small voice.

"I told them about last night," Scottie said. "About what you did. They wanted to see where it happened."

"But I didn't do it!" Garry protested. "See?" He held up the third match. "It burned out on top of the boulder when I dropped it! I didn't start the fire!"

The firefighter and the coaches exchanged looks. "You were lighting matches out here last night?" the firefighter said at last.

Garry gulped and slowly lowered his hand. "I-I — yes. But you knew that already, didn't you?" He turned to Scottie. "Isn't that what you told them? That I started the fire?"

"Huh?" Scottie shook his head. "Why would I think you started the fire?"

"Because you found the matches in my sweatshirt pocket!"

Scottie raised and lowered his shoulders. "I didn't find any matches, Garry. We're out here so I can show them where you rescued me from the river!"

The firefighter stepped forward then. "Perhaps you boys better walk us through what went on here last night. Maybe we'll be able to piece together this puzzle once and for all."

14

Garry was still confused but he did as the firefighter asked. "I found a box of matches under a bucket," he said. "I lit three of them."

He shot a quick glance at the coaches and the fireman. "I know I shouldn't have, but I did it up on the rock where they wouldn't burn anything."

The chief let out a sigh of annoyance. "Son, what you did could have caused a whole peck of trouble — for you and for the forest. Now tell me the truth, did you light more than three?"

Garry shook his head vehemently. "No, sir!

I only lit those three, two on the strike plate and the third on the rock's surface when the strike plate wore down. I swear! Then I heard Scottie call my name and started running toward the river."

"Show me the path you took," the chief instructed.

"This way," Garry said, hurrying down the trail as he had the night before. "See that root? I tripped over it. Look, you can even see where I hit the dirt."

He pointed to a gouge in the mud and to the skid mark on his sweatshirt. A sudden thought crossed his mind. *Maybe the match-box fell out of my pocket when I fell. But if it did, then how did Michael get it?*

A question from the fire chief interrupted his thoughts. "What happened next, after you fell?"

"I went through this thicket" — Garry

pushed his way through the brush as he had before — "and saw Scottie there, in the river."

The fire chief followed him through the thicket. He looked at the river for a long moment. Then he glanced back toward the boulder. He seemed to be considering something. When he spoke at last, it wasn't to Garry, it was to Scottie.

"Why did you call to Garry?" he asked.

"I was trying to get his attention," Scottie replied.

"How did you know he was out here?"

To Garry's surprise, Scottie pointed to a place on the far riverbank. "I saw him over there. That's why I was trying to cross the river — to get over to him."

Garry started to protest that he'd never set foot on that side, but the fire chief raised a hand to keep him quiet.

"Are you certain?" the chief asked quietly. "Because Garry just told us he was on the boulder when he heard you call."

Scottie blinked in confusion. "I-I thought I saw him. He had on a Rockets sweatshirt." He turned thoughtful. "But come to think of it, I never saw his face because he had his hood up."

Garry gave a sharp cry. "But my sweatshirt doesn't have a hood! I cut it off! See?" He held up his sweatshirt for the chief to inspect.

Scottie grabbed Garry's arm then. "Wait a sec! Remember how I asked how you got to me so quickly?"

"Yeah, so?" Then Garry's eyes widened as he realized what Scottie was driving at. "You thought I had crossed the river and reappeared here, which would have been impossible in that short amount of time! But it wasn't me, it was someone in a hooded sweatshirt!"

"Hold on," Coach Hasbrouck interjected. "Are you saying there was another Rocket out here?"

Scottie nodded vigorously. "There must have been."

"Could you identify him?"

The Thunder goalkeeper thought for a moment and then shook his head. "I only saw him for a second. Then I slipped on the rock and fell in the water."

But Garry had been thinking hard. Now he cleared his throat. "Um, Coach, I think I might know who it was."

They all looked at him.

"If I did drop those matches when I tripped, then the other person who was out here could have found them. He could even have started the fire."

"Go on," Coach Hasbrouck encouraged.

Garry bit his lip. "Michael has the matches, sir. He showed me the box just a little while ago. And he owns a Rockets sweatshirt like mine. Only his has a hood on it still."

The coach blew out a long breath. "Garry, what you are saying is very serious. And I know that you and Michael don't get along."

"Coach," Garry said urgently, "I'm not making it up just to get Michael in trouble. Honest! Ask Michael about those matches if you don't believe me!"

"Unfortunately, son, it would be your word against his," the Thunder coach pointed out. "As grateful to you as I am for rescuing Scottie here, I'm not sure who I'd believe — the boy who's just confessed to lighting matches in the woods, or the boy who reported the fire. There's no proof that this Michael was out here or that he even has the matches!"

"But the figure in the hooded sweat-shirt —" Garry began.

"— could have been anyone," Coach Has-brouck finished.

15

The group left the woods soon after, having come to no final conclusions about the matter. Garry returned to his cabin and lay down on his bunk feeling completely dejected.

Well, at least one good thing came out of this, he thought sourly. *Now that I've confessed, I won't have to help Michael get that top scorer award.*

Then he sat up, thinking. A slow smile crossed his lips.

If I don't feed him the ball the next game, he'll rat me out! "And to do that," he whispered triumphantly, "he'll have to show the coach the matches!"

Convinced that his plan would work, he jumped down from his bunk and set off to talk to his teammates — not to urge them to feed Michael the ball, as Michael had ordered him to do, but to ask them to do just the opposite!

The Rockets were scheduled to play the Bears right after lunch. Garry managed to explain the situation to Jeff and Todd and a few other teammates by then. He asked them to keep quiet to Michael's loyal supporters, however — particularly Evan. They all agreed to help out.

Garry came to the field determined to play the best game of his life. But he put on a morose face so that Michael wouldn't suspect anything. He spotted Scottie in the bleachers and hurried over to tell him what was happening too.

"Good luck, man, I'll be rooting for you!" Scottie said.

Garry did his warm-up exercises with the rest of the team and then, when the referee blew a blast on his whistle, ran to his place in the wing area for the start of the game. Michael sauntered past him, shot him with a finger gun, and continued on to the center X.

"In your dreams, Donofrio," Garry muttered.

The referee placed the ball between the Bears center attacker and Michael. He trotted back out of the way and blew another whistle blast. The game was on!

Michael usually had a quick stick on the face-off but this Bear was quicker. He raked the ball away before Michael could even flip his stick. Then, when Michael tried to poke it away, the Bear sent it rocketing through the grass to his teammate.

Garry charged out of the wing area, leveled his stick at the Bears ball carrier, and jabbed it at the shaft of his opponent's stick. But the Bear twisted away and slashed his stick downward in an attempted pass back to his center. Unfortunately for him, he released the ball too late. Instead of flying through the air it struck the grass with a loud *thud* and bounced up and away, free to anyone who could get a stick on it.

That "anyone" wound up being Jeff. He caught it in his pocket on midbounce, darted around the Bears frustrated attacker, and fired a pass to Conor.

"Here!" Michael screamed. "Pass it here!"

Conor squared off as if to send it in Michael's direction. Michael took off, holding up his stick to make an over-the-shoulder catch. But the pass never came, for after squaring off, Conor pivoted on one foot and lobbed the ball back to Jeff.

Michael, meanwhile, continued to run, holding his stick aloft like a standard-bearer holding a flag. When the ball didn't come, he looked back and nearly collided with a Bears defender.

"Watch it, buddy, will ya?" the Bear growled just as Jeff flipped the ball over to Garry.

"Give it here, Wallis — or else!" Michael yelled.

Garry ignored him. He looked to Conor. Conor wasn't open. Samuel was covered too, and Jeff was too far behind to send the ball there. That left Garry with three choices: keep the ball and hope he could get a shot off on goal; pass to Evan, who was coming up behind him; or pass to Michael, who was still yelling at him.

The decision was taken out of his hands when a Bears defender ran forward and stuck himself to Garry like glue. Since Garry refused to pass to Michael, he sent the ball back to Evan.

"It'll reach Michael anyhow," he muttered.

But to his surprise, Evan didn't automatically toss the ball to Michael. Rather, he twisted away from a Bears midfielder and fired the ball to Jeff, who was so surprised he nearly missed the catch.

But he managed to control it and get it to Conor. Conor's stick whistled through the air as he slashed it sideways and rocketed the ball past the goalkeeper into the net. Goal!

"Yee-haa!" Conor leaped and twirled in midair, drawing laughs from the sidelines and his teammates. Only the Bears were silent.

They didn't stay quiet for long, however, for once again the Bears center attacker took possession on the face-off. This time, he carried the ball halfway down the field before the Rockets midfielders could catch up to him. Jeff and Samuel double-teamed him but the Bear outfoxed them both, twisting away to feed the ball over to the attacker on his right.

Brandon was caught napping. The Bear barreled past him and confronted Christopher. The two mirrored one another for a moment before the Bear faked a throw that sent Christopher moving in the wrong direction. From there, it was just one swift, accurate throw and the Bears had tied it up 1–1.

As Garry headed back to the wing area for the face-off, he fully expected Michael to threaten him once again. He wasn't disappointed.

"I'm warning you, Wallis," the center attacker hissed. "Get me the ball or —"

"Lay off, Donofrio, will you?"

Garry's jaw dropped in amazement. The retort hadn't come from Jeff, or Conor, or even Carl.

It had come from Evan!

16

Evan's moment of defiance toward Michael was astonishing — and more amazingly, it wasn't his last that game!

Over and over, Michael all but ordered his most loyal lapdog to feed him the ball. And over and over, Evan sent the ball elsewhere. Michael, so used to simply taking the ball and running with it, spent much of his time dancing about in frustration with an empty pocket.

The Rockets, meanwhile, were busy working different plays the coach had taught them during countless practices. Before long, it became obvious to them — and to many of those watching the game — that Michael didn't have a clue how those plays were supposed to go.

"Michael, you're supposed to run *behind* the net, not in *front* of it," Evan bellowed after one botched play turned into a fast break — and a successful goal — for the Bears.

"If I didn't know any better," Garry whispered to his brother as they hurried off the field for the halftime break, "I'd say Evan has a grudge against Michael!"

"It does seem like there is trouble in paradise!" Todd whispered back.

The trouble got worse — for Michael, anyway. When the second half began, the once-unstoppable attacker was left sitting on the bench while Todd took the face-off!

Todd might not have been a dynamo like Michael, but he was a complete team player.

So was Pedro, who came off the bench to take Conor's place. Together, the two subs moved the ball down the field so smoothly it looked like they were doing a simple passing drill. And when Todd slashed his stick downward and sent the ball into the lower right corner of the net to put the Rockets ahead by one, no one cheered louder than Garry.

And to think Michael wanted him off the team! he thought as he smiled proudly at Todd.

But that one-point advantage didn't last long. The Bears controlled the ball after the next face-off and roared down the field in an all-out blitz on the goal. Carl and Eric stood their ground but Andrew, subbing for Brandon, hesitated in the face of the onslaught. When he did finally move to cover his man, it was too late. The Bear, a huge but fleet-footed boy, blew by him with the ball safely cradled in his stick pocket.

Christopher came out of the goal to cut him off, but when he did, another Bear sidled in, received a pass, and angled the ball past the Rockets goalie. Tied game again.

The score stayed even throughout the third quarter, and into the fourth. Garry was beginning to wonder if either team would ever break through when Samuel got the ball and yelled, "Middie sweep!"

The Rockets had tried the play a few times earlier in the game without success. But that was when Michael had still been on the field. This time, Todd was in the center attacker spot. Garry wondered for a split second if his brother, usually a midfielder, would know how to run the play from that position.

He needn't have worried. When not playing lacrosse, Todd liked to play elaborate magician-and-monster role-playing games. To play games like that well, he had to know what each piece was up to at all times and keep track of his opponent's action too. Now, Todd transferred those skills to the lacrosse field.

He planted himself at the top of the crease, ready to screen for Samuel. Samuel darted by him and looked to the goal, but even with Todd blocking the goalie's view, he didn't have a clear shot.

Now the ball went to Jeff. Once more, Todd set a screen — and this time, the play worked like a charm. Jeff darted to one side of Todd and laced in a perfect shot seconds before the goalie realized what he was up to.

The Rockets were up by one! That late-game goal seemed to deflate the Bears. When the game ended a few minutes later, the Rockets had pushed yet another goal across the line to win by two.

Garry cheered with the rest of his team

and then, winded from playing the entire game, headed to the bench for a much-needed rest. But any thought of relaxing went out the window when Michael planted himself on the bench beside him.

"You are really in for it, you know that?" the attacker threatened. "If I don't score several times the next game, you are *dead!*"

Garry took off his helmet, ran his fingers through his sweaty hair, and put on a puzzled look. "Correct me if I'm wrong, but don't you actually have to be in the game in order to score?"

Garry had often heard the expression "so angry his head exploded." But he didn't really get what it meant until just then. Michael's eyes bugged out, his nostrils flared, his face turned beet red, and his lips pulled back in a snarl. Garry actually leaned back, certain his nemesis was about to lose it completely.

But Michael just stood up and shook a finger in Garry's face. "You just kissed your place on this team goodbye, Wallis!"

He whirled around and thundered over to Coach Hasbrouck. "Coach, I have something I think you, and the authorities, will be *very* interested in seeing!" he cried. With a triumphant flourish, he reached into his duffel bag and pulled out the matchbox.

The coach looked at the box for a long moment. "You know, Michael," he said finally, "I think you're right. I think the authorities are going to be very interested in seeing this. But tell me something first."

He fixed the boy with a steely stare. "Where exactly did you get these matches, and why are you carrying them around in your duffel bag?"

17

Michael blinked. He opened his mouth, closed it, and then opened it again. At last, he jerked a thumb at Garry.

"They're his!" he blurted. "He's the one who started the fire!"

"You saw him?" the coach asked calmly.

Now Michael puffed out his chest. "I sure did! He was lighting matches up on that big boulder! And . . . and . . ." Suddenly, he faltered.

"And?" Coach Hasbrouck prompted.

Now Michael clamped his mouth shut and didn't open it.

"I'll tell you what happened, Coach," came a new voice.

Garry stared at the speaker, dumbfounded. "Evan?"

Several other Rockets looked up with interest.

"E-man, my friend, what're you doing?" Michael said.

Evan held up a hand in warning. "Don't 'E-man' me, Donofrio. I'm sick and tired of you and your stupid mind games!"

That caught the Rockets' full attention. They gathered around to listen to what Evan had to say. Scottie came over from the stands too.

Evan turned back to the coach. "I was with him the other night in the woods. We followed Garry out there." He shot Garry a quick look of apology. "I honestly don't know what Michael planned to do if we found you. I just hope I would have had the guts to stop him if . . . well, you know."

Garry nodded grimly.

"Anyway, when we didn't find you right away, we split up. I went on one side of the river, Michael went on the other." Now Evan looked at Scottie. "You thought I was Garry, didn't you? When you shouted his name, I panicked and ran farther up the river. There's a little footbridge up there. I crossed over and headed down the other side. That's when I saw Michael light the match."

"It's a lie!" Michael yelled suddenly. He rounded on Evan. "You're the one who lit the match, not me!"

Evan shook his head. "No, *I'm* the one who grabbed the cell phone from your sweatshirt pocket and called 9-1-1! *You're* the one who freaked out when your match accidentally

121

landed in that pile of sticks! You ran away, leaving me to deal with the flames!"

"Prove it!" Michael challenged.

At this, Evan grew silent. "I can't," he said finally.

Michael snorted. "Then it's your word against mine, isn't it?"

At this, the coach cleared his throat. "Actually, it may be Evan's *words* against yours." When everyone looked at him in confusion, he explained. "Emergency calls are recorded. That's probably why the fire chief thought Michael had made the call, because Michael's cell phone number showed up on the caller identification. But if we can hear the actual recording —"

"— we'll hear Evan's voice, not Michael's!" Garry finished excitedly.

Coach Hasbrouck nodded. "I think you two boys better come along with me to the fire station," he said to Michael and Evan. "I'll want the chief to hear your stories. The rest of you, shower up and get some dinner. Oh, and good game, Rockets!"

Garry, Scottie, and the rest of the Rockets murmured their thanks as the coach placed a firm hand on Michael's shoulder and led him away. Evan followed.

"Wow," Garry said after they'd gone. "That was . . ." But he couldn't come up with a word to describe it.

"What do you suppose turned Evan against Michael?" Todd asked. "I mean, come on, he's put up with so much from him for so long!"

Jeff screwed up his face as if in deep thought. "If I had to guess," he mused, "I'd say the break came when Michael proclaimed himself a hero on that stage. I mean, it was hard enough for *us* to listen to. If Michael really ran from the fire like Evan said he did, think of how hard it must have been for Evan to stomach!"

They all broke out laughing at that image. "Speaking of stomach," Garry said when they'd calmed down, "I'm famished! How about some dinner?"

They gathered their gear and began to walk toward their cabin. Scottie went with them. All at once, Garry stopped and grabbed the Thunder goalkeeper by the arm.

"There's something I've been meaning to ask you. When we played you yesterday, how did I get so many goals past you? And how did you stop so many of Michael's shots? Usually he's chalking them up left and right!"

Scottie grinned. "Bet he was pretty PO'd, wasn't he?"

Garry nodded. "Yeah. In fact, he accused you of letting me score."

Now Scottie laughed out loud. "And risk losing the game? Fat chance! I stopped Michael cold because I knew every time he got the ball near the goal he was going to try to score. It's pretty easy to defend against someone when you know what they're going to do. You? I couldn't read you. *That's* why you scored."

Garry gave him a sidelong glance. "Did that make you mad? Because you wouldn't even look at me after the game. That's when I thought that *you* thought I'd started the fire."

"Naw. I was just down because we'd lost the game!" With that, he thumped Garry on the back and departed.

Then Todd fell back and motioned for Garry to join him. His face was serious.

"Garry," he said, "you are one lucky kid, you know that? What if . . . ?" He let his voice trail away, but his gaze was intent.

"I know, it was a really stupid move, lighting those matches," Garry replied. "Believe me, I've learned my lesson. It's a huge mistake to play with fire, whether it's the kind that burns wood" — he tapped his chest — "or the kind that burns here when you're angry. From now on, if I need to lose my cool, I'll find a better way to do it!"

Todd's face cleared. "Good. Now, let's put that whole thing behind us and focus on what's important!"

"Winning the tournament?" Garry guessed.

"No! Dinner! Come on, I'm starved!"

Matt Christopher®

Muhammad Ali

Lance Armstrong

Kobe Bryant

Jennifer Capriati

Dale Earnhardt Sr.

Jeff Gordon

Ken Griffey Jr.

Mia Hamm

Tony Hawk

Ichiro

Derek Jeter

Randy Johnson

Michael Jordan

Yao Ming

Shaquille O'Neal

Jackie Robinson

Alex Rodriguez

Babe Ruth

Curt Schilling

Sammy Sosa

Tiger Woods

Read them all!

*Previously published as Crackerjack Halfback

All available in paperback from Little, Brown and Company

**Previously published as Pressure Play

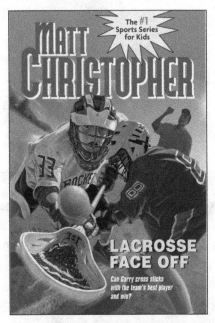

TWO PLAYERS, ONE DREAM...
to win the Little League Baseball® World Series

Read all about Carter's and Liam's journeys in the Little League series
by **MATT CHRISTOPHER**.

Ⓛ Ⓑ **LITTLE, BROWN AND COMPANY**
BOOKS FOR YOUNG READERS

Discover more at **lb-kids.com**

GET ON THE FIELD, UNDER THE NET, AND BEHIND THE PLATE WITH YOUR
FAVORITE ALL-STARS!

Read the entire Great Americans in Sports series by
MATT CHRISTOPHER

9 780316 016315